On loan from

SCHOOL
LIBRARIES
RESOURCES
SERVICE

TH⠀⠀⠀⠀⠀⠀⠀⠀⠀GS TO:

Telephone 020 8200 8948
Fax⠀⠀⠀⠀020 8201 3018
E-mail⠀⠀⠀slrs@barnet.gov.uk

BARNET
LONDON BOROUGH

For Ace, who knows
a thing or two about crazy hair

First published 2003 by Walker Books Ltd
87 Vauxhall Walk, London SE11 5HJ

2 4 6 8 10 9 7 5 3 1

© 2003 Barney Saltzberg

This book has been typeset in Maiandra

Printed in China

British Library Cataloguing in Publication Data:
a catalogue record for this book
is available from the British Library

ISBN 0-7445-9344-1

CRAZY HAIR DAY

BARNEY SALTZBERG

WALKER BOOKS
AND SUBSIDIARIES
LONDON • BOSTON • SYDNEY

Stanley Birdbaum woke up early. Bald Eagle Primary School was holding a Crazy Hair Day and Stanley couldn't wait. His school had held a Pyjama Day, a Sixties Day and a Twin Day. Stanley's favourite had been Twin Day because he and his best friend, Larry Finchfeather, had worn exactly the same thing.

Stanley was ready. He had elastic bands. He had styling gel. And to make his hair perfect, Stanley had two cans of Hallowe'en hair spray.

Stanley's mother knew just what to do. She wrapped. She dipped. And to make his hair perfect, she sprayed Stanley's hair bright orange and blue.

"Ta-da!" said Stanley. "*I* am a work of art!"

"*You* are going to be late if you don't hurry!"
said his mother.

Stanley rolled the elastic bands in his hair.
He gently tapped the tops of his spikes.

"This," he said, "is going to be a day I will
never forget."

I expect Larry Finchfeather and I will have the craziest hair in the whole school! Stanley thought.

As he walked towards the classroom, he heard his teacher talking.

"And remember," Mr Winger was saying, "Crazy Hair Day is ...

next
Friday."

Everybody stopped.
Everybody stared.
Stanley felt sick.

Larry Finchfeather said,
"Is that a hair-do or
a hair-don't?"

Everybody laughed.
Stanley ran to the
toilets.

A few minutes later, Stanley heard someone come in.
"It's me, Larry!"

"The Larry Finchfeather who just made fun of me
in front of the whole class?" asked Stanley.

"I was only teasing!" said Larry.

"Sometimes you tease me too much," said Stanley.

"Mr Winger said he wants me to try to be a
    peacemaker instead of a troublemaker," said Larry.
"I'm supposed to bring you back to class."

"I'm not going!" said Stanley.

"If you stay in here, you'll miss being in the class photo!" said Larry.

"I thought that was next Friday!" said Stanley.

"Crazy Hair Day is next Friday," Larry said.
"Today is School Photo Day."

Stanley rolled the elastic bands in his hair. He gently tapped the tops of his spikes.

"This," he said, "is going to be a day I will never forget."

Larry suggested that Stanley tried washing his hair in the sink.

"It won't help," said Stanley. "Hallowe'en hair colour lasts for days."

"Well, it really doesn't matter. It's only your hair," Larry told him. "If you don't come out of here by the end of maths, I'm coming to get you. You can't stay in here all day."

It was very quiet after Larry had left, and Stanley
wondered whether he really *could* spend
all day in the toilets.

He ate his lunch.

He drew pictures.

He even timed himself to
see how fast he could flush
all the toilets.
"Thirty-two-and-a-half
seconds!" he shouted.
"A new world record by me,
Stanley Birdbaum!"

Stanley had counted up
to one hundred and
twenty-one,

one hundred and
twenty-two,

one hundred and
twenty-three drops of water
from a leaky tap when
Larry Finchfeather
came back.

"Beep! Time's up. Let's go," Larry announced.
"Photo time!"

"If I'm in it, I'll look like the class weirdo!"
said Stanley.

"Remember Sixties Day, when Mr Winger had flu
but came in anyway?" said Larry. "He said the day
wouldn't be the same if we weren't all together.
You have to come; I'll give you five minutes."

After Larry Finchfeather had left,
Stanley Birdbaum thought about
Sixties Day when Mr Winger had
taught them all those great old songs.

He remembered how on Pyjama Day everybody in his class had worn pyjamas and slippers.

Then Stanley imagined what his class photo would look like without him.

He decided to go back to his classroom.
To keep from being nervous,
Stanley made up a song:
Crazy hair, crazy hair.
How I wish it wasn't there.

Stanley felt someone touch his shoulder. "I was just coming to get you," said Larry Finchfeather.

"What if they laugh at me again?" asked Stanley.

"Everything will be fine," Larry whispered. "I promise!"

Stanley stood in front of his class.

Everybody stopped. Everybody stared.

Stanley rolled the elastic bands in his hair.
He gently tapped the tops of his spikes…

"This," he said, "is going to be a day...

I will never forget!"